A WORLD OF WEIRD TRUTHS AND TRUTHFUL WEIRDNESSES

Else Cederborg

authorHOUSE®

AuthorHouse™ UK Ltd.
500 Avebury Boulevard
Central Milton Keynes, MK9 2BE
www.authorhouse.co.uk
Phone: 08001974150

First published by AuthorHouse 10/07/2011

ISBN: 978-1-4567-7689-3 (sc)
ISBN: 978-1-4567-7688-6 (ebk)

CONTENTS

III. The Weird World of Reality: Ezine-Articles   85

I. Fantastic Tales, Fables and Stories of Realities Beyond Reality

1. Pictures On A Train:

As I enter the train I notice at once that only one seat isn't in use already. Strangely enough several passengers are standing up on their feet, although swaying to the somewhat abrupt movements of the train. Still, nobody seems to be interested in this particular seat.

These compartments on old trains hold five groups of four seats facing each other. I sense that this particular corner of the compartment is special as none of the standing and presumably tired passengers has claimed one of the four seats. Three of them are taken by one lonely passenger and has been marked down as occupied by the stuff he has put on two of the seats. As he is sitting in the third one only one of the four seats is free. However, it's obvious that this seat and this part of the compartment isn't exactly popular with the other passengers. No one as much as looks at him or glances in his direction, and no one as much as eyes the seats. It's as if he is invisible. However, after a while I sense that his presence is felt by everyone, including me.

Being tired and with sore feet from too much walking I decide to sit down in the empty seat. As I do the strange man, sitting opposite me, lifts his head a little, but I don't have the feeling that he looks at me. – Perhaps he is blind,

1

I think to myself. Anyway, blind or not he has conquered three seats on a train full of people looking exhausted. Quite an exploit these days ...

Now that I sit so close to him I can't help noticing that his hands move dexterously behind a newspaper and I realize that what I thought was debris is cuttings from the mass of newspapers that are piled up in one of the seats. Somehow it amuses me that he is the conqueror of three seats in an overloaded train, but that all he does is to cut out whatever he finds interesting in these newspapers. Had he put up his feet or something like that I might have understood him and so would many, many of his exhausted fellow passengers. Now they only understand that this is a shady character, someone one shouldn't upset or even notice.

Sometimes the clipping movements behind the newspaper stops for a while and one of his hands shoots out in a fast movement to put a new paper clipping on top of the pile on the empty seat. All of these clippings look like nonsense to me as they don't represent pictures in full. No headlines, no graphics, only a part of an article of some kind. I realize that the reason for this is that he has built his pile upside down so that all the pictures face downwards: As each clipping is lying upside down I only catch a word or part of a picture from articles that he has cut through to get what's on the other side of the clipping.

However, suddenly he makes a mistake and puts a clipping face upward. At first I can't see what it is – or rather, my instinct tells me not to try to do so as it starts to dawn upon me what it is he is collecting: Eyes, I see eyes, and when he gets confused after his mistake and turns the entire pile face up for some minutes I see more eyes, I see noses, and I see mouths.

Suddenly all of these facial details, cut out of the newspapers, take on another meaning. Something I saw years back, something with blood and even a stench on them. Yes, this is a slaughterhouse, only in paper and without the genuine stench from the blood and the intestines. Nevertheless, a slaughterhouse, and I think that I recognize the eyes and other severed facial traits of celebrities like e.g. Angelina Jolie, George Clooney, Obama, The Pope, Brad Pitt and many other famous or just pretty people.

When I look up in bewilderment at this sight I see that all of a sudden he is staring at me. His large and sort of oblong eyes are like made in glass, very much like sea water, mirroring the clouded sky just before the thunder sets in ....

2. Giraffe, Giraffe ...

Once there was a giraffe, Oliver, who had a very short neck. Now, with giraffes there is a rule that they look alike, but this one looked very different from the others.

"Stretch! Stretch, Ollie," his worried Mom said, and he did, but it didn't do much to get him to grow.

"I'm small," he wailed, being somewhat of a cry-baby, "the others laugh at me." That was only too true, they did laugh at him, even his beloved Belinda who had an excellent size neck and loved to flaunt it in front of all her young admirers. She nibbled leaves from the top of the trees whereas Oliver had to make do with the middle branches. Not that that was so very bad because now he had them to himself and they were just as tasty as the other ones. Something he didn't think of as all he had on his mind was his looks which even he found very strange indeed.

He couldn't help himself, but simply had to talk to other animals about his neck and to ask them to evaluate his looks although he wasn't too sure about the honesty of their answers.

"Oh," the lion said, "I wouldn't worry about that. To me you look excellent. A real ... eh' ... treat ..."

One drop of saliva left its mouth as it said this, but Oliver didn't see it, all he had on his mind was his "excellent looks". Still, the lion was only one animal so he also asked the crocodile. This sneaky creature looked at him with unflinching eyes and then it said: "A bit small, but still, bigger than a monkey. Very good looks, very good indeed ..."

Oliver felt relieved by this comment on his looks, but found that he also needed the opinion of the hippopotamus.

Now, this was a very big and sulking creature who loved to deride what he didn't have himself.

"Your neck is real pretty. It looks more like mine than the necks of the other giraffes. As to the rest it's very giraffish, all too long legs, a couple of ridiculous horns and so on. Besides, your eyes are much too big and those long eyelashes make you look drowsy. However, your neck is real pretty for a giraffe."

Oliver was dumbfounded. His neck looked more like in a hippo than in a giraffe?!!!! Disaster! He got so shocked that he simply turned on his heel and left without thanking the blunt hippopotamus for his opinion.

For some time Oliver hid in shame from his fellow giraffes, but it was a dangerous way of living as he, being alone, lacked the protection of the flock. However, it did teach him some truths about the feline mind that he brought to good use when he grew up to become a young adult, looking for love and appreciation in the female beauties of his flock. He learnt to outsmart a hungry lion or leopard, to dodge all assaults and to stay alive by using his own, hard won streetwise skills.

When the Springtime made his memories of Belinda and the other young females dawn upon him he wanted to reunite with the flock and that was done very fast by the assistance of his doting Mom. She loved her son, short-necked or not, and always wanted to help him out.

However, shortly afterwards a situation arose in which she couldn't do anything to help him: He was attacked by Brutus, another one of Belinda's many admirers. Brutus had a loooong neck and fine horns and he knew how to use both: He struck the necks of his opponents by ramming his own neck into them, over and over again. Being very strong he used to win these combats, but not this time. When he struck out he had set his strike for someone with the usual long giraffe neck. That meant that although targeting Oliver he didn't hit him.

"What!?" Brutus exclaimed when Oliver hit him at a much lower part of his neck than he was used to in these combats. It hurt like nothing before and he started to cough to get his breathing back on track. That's when Oliver struck him the second time and then, after only two strikes, won the combat.

Every giraffe in the flock was surprised. Some even shocked because of Oliver's odd looks that used to set him apart as a born loser. However, he had won, and for once he could prance in front of the females, showing off his short, but efficient neck. It sure made them get their eyes up for the charm of short guys and teach all of them a lesson.

3. Lions in the Home

Jennifer heard the heavy panting and knew that she had to get out of the room as fast as possible. She couldn't see the animal, but the subdued growling told her that this would be a large feline of some sort. The sound came from the area in front of the three windows and she suddenly remembered that she hadn't closed the middle one. It came as a shock to her that she herself might have let in her assailant – and assailed she would be if she didn't get out – whatever the creature was. A pungent smell hit her nostrils and she realized that the animal by now was very close to her hiding place behind the couch. In the same moment she felt the heavy paw on her thigh she rolled, lying full length on the floor, right over to the door. Somehow she got out and even succeeded in closing the door behind her. This narrow escape led to a roar of disappointment from the other side of the closed door – and then she awoke, drained mentally with fright and soaked in sweat.

Slowly she sat up in bed, looking down at herself and her sweat-soaked nightie.

– Nothing to see today, she thought, heaving a sigh of relief. Then she caught sight of a small rip in the thin fabric. – Oh no, she thought, not that ...

As she sat staring at the rift the door opened and her mother came into the room.

"Good morning, darling?" she said. "Did you sleep well?"

Jennifer looked at her with dark, worried eyes which spoke volumes about nightly horrors.

"Oh dear, you ought to go and see doctor Rita so that you can get something to sleep on. It's too bad that

7

you should have all these nightmares. What was it this time?"

Jennifer told her about the growling, the reek and the big paw.

"How strange," her mother said, "why should you dream of this kind of dangers? You've never ever met a lion or tiger outside of documentaries on television and in the Zoo. Now they seem to inhabit your home at night. Very strange."

Jennifer agreed, it really was strange that these animals should appear in her sitting-room, bath-room, kitchen or study every night. The only place she hadn't met them was in her bedroom and still that was where she dreamt of them. Once she had fallen asleep on the couch in the sitting-room and then she had met something that looked like a cheetah in the kitchen, but not the room where she in reality was.

"OK," she said, "enough is enough so I shall go and see my doctor although I don't expect much to come from it. What could she do except giving me some medicine to make me sleep?"

Her mother didn't answer, but she looked at her with a very worried expression in her eyes. All this seemed so weird to her as she, as far as she knew, had never had a nightmare in all her life.

That same day Jennifer went to see her doctor, actually her cousin, Rita. She told her about the strange occurrences and she also mentioned the rifts and tears she had noticed in her nighties.

"I've bought so many new ones," she said, "and somehow they too get torn."

"I hope you realize that you do it to yourself," Rita said in a stern voice.

"No, but I knew you would say something like that," Jennifer said in a teasing voice. "You always do ..."

"Well, being a doctor I have to keep my sanity ..."

"And I've lost mine?"

"No-no-no, but haven't you eaten something right before going to sleep? Or what about watching Animal Planet or Discovery at a late hour?"

"None of that," Jennifer said. "I never watch any animal programs out of fear for having those dreams. However, they come anyway and now it's every night."

Rita sat still for a while, then she said: "OK, there are no simple explanations to this phenomenon, but lately the technique of "Imagery rehearsal" has become popular, maybe you should try that out ..."

"Is it any good?"

"It has been of help to many people, but I think it shall be difficult to get started on a treatment right away. Perhaps in 4-6 month or so ..."

"That long? Then I must have something to sleep on as I really need my sleep."

"Yes, even though I don't like it, you shall have something, and then I shall see to it that you may start on the "Imagery rehearsal" as soon as possible."

"Thanks," Jennifer said, "but what are nightmares in your opinion?"

"We don't really know, but there are a lot of theories about them. Some say that they come from stress or post-traumatic experiences, but you're not stressed, are you?"

"No," Jennifer said, "I'm not. Neither overworked, depressed or anything like that, but I'm p..... off at this nightly show of claws and fangs from nowhere."

"Well, take a pill or two and phone me next week."

As Jennifer left she felt hopeful. Rita was a good doctor and also a good cousin. She would find a way to stop this nonsense. Then she came to think of those tears and rifts in her nighties and she got annoyed at the idea that she had made them herself. Besides, she suddenly felt the

9

large paw on her thigh once more and saw the rift as if both were happening at that very moment.

Before going to sleep she took one pill and when she woke up in the morning she felt relieved: No big animals, no fear and no hazardous escapes, only a restful sleep all night. However, when she removed her nightie she saw a new rift and beneath it there was a fresh, but small wound. She stared at both in disbelief, but then she decided that she must have torn it in her sleep as well as hurting herself.

For a week she slept like a log every night, but woke up to new damages to her clothes and to herself. She decided not to tell Rita about these mishaps, but instead stress the fact that she didn't have those scary dreams anymore. The same night she once more felt the presence of the big felines and smelled the reek of carnivores. She found it OK to start on a dose of two pills instead of one and for some weeks she didn't experience those nocturnal meetings with predatory cats.

– So that's the answer to the problem, she thought. More and more pills, even though I ordinarily never take any. She hated the idea of having to discuss the matter with Rita once more so she decided to make some experiences on her own: She had a couple of nice, rich sandwiches right before bedtime after having watched Animal Planet, Discovery and National Geographic for some hours and she didn't take any pills.

Soon she felt the presence of the big feline, but this time she seemed to be in the middle of the pride of several animals. Claws and fangs to all sides of her, growls and roars as well as the strong smell of carnivores told her that her fear of not being able to steer her dreams had come true. As one of the lions (or whatever it was) brushed by her she felt its fur strike sparks against her thin nightie. It let out a roar right into her face and she fled out the room. This time she was followed by the animal which was right behind her. When she woke up in the early hours her nightie was torn and she had something which looked like clawmarks on her legs.

That day she phoned Rita and asked her about the "Imagery Rehearsal"-program. However, now her cousin wasn't too optimistic about the treatment anymore. She told her that there had been a disappointment in this method, but that if she wanted to give it a try she would back her up and help her out.

Jennifer thanked her, but she didn't commit herself to anything. "I shall think it over once more," she said, "but if you say it's no good then I shall most probably not try it out."

The same night she found herself lying on the sun-drenched ground in the pride of the lions. She felt jaws close on her legs and arms, claws tearing her chest and throat right before her mother woke her up, very worried at her high-pitched screams.

"Oh dear, I thought you had stopped those nightmares with the medicine ...." she said.

Jennifer didn't answer, all she was able to do was to sit up, bury her tear-drenched face in her hands and cry and cry and cry. Then she caught sight of her totally torn nightie and her bloodied legs and arms. She let out a scream, jumped out of bed and ran to the windows. Without any hesitation, and before her mother could stop her, she flung herself out the middle one.

Some months later one of the new owners of the flat, Katherine, had a strange dream of snakes. A big snake was lying on top of her chest, its tongue spilling in its mouth. When she woke up her husband, James, consoled her and they had a loving talk about nightmares that ended up in passionate love-making. However, when Katherine had another dream of snakes the night after James couldn't help being a bit annoyed. After all he had to sleep well to perform well in his job as a teacher.

Night after night, Katherine dreamt om snakes. When she one night was visited by a 6 metres long King Cobra that was the end of the marriage. They had a vehement fight and she moved out of the flat – never to dream of snakes again.

However that same night James had a most vivid dream of sharks. Somehow he had been transported to an underwater-world of ferocious predators with jaws like nothing else in the world. As he stared into the cold eyes of the sharks he felt a fear that went like a spear up his spine to penetrate his brain.

4. The Petrified Woman

When Rosa woke up in the morning she felt like all her muscles had frozen. It was very painful to get out of bed and she moaned when she fought to sit down on the toilet. Her husband, Stephen, called out to her through the locked door: "Are you hurt, did you stumble or what's wrong?"

"I don't know," she said, "it hurts and my muscles are all cramped together."

Afterwards, when she joined him in the kitchen, she felt nauseated by the sheer thought of food. "It must be the flu," she said, "and I don't think I should go to work today, also because it's contagious."

"That's OK," he said, both being her boss and her husband. "I shall get Catherine to take over for you."

Rosa hated the very idea of Catherine taking over for her as she felt that the pretty, young girl would love to take everything, including Stephen, if she got the chance. However, feeling this miserable she didn't have much extra energy to fight this solution so she didn't answer him.

Stephen knew full well that Rosa hated Catherine and he had only mentioned this solution to make her pull herself together and go to work. When she didn't take the bait he realized that she really felt miserable. – My God, he thought to himself, could she really be this ill? So it seemed as she staggered back to bed without eating anything.

As to Rosa she felt how her muscles got more and more sore as well as stiffer and stiffer by each step. When she finally made it to her bed she couldn't keep back her tears anymore, but cried with pain. Only that too hurt and she ended up realizing that the only solution was to be quite still, not move at all and had she been able to breathe without moving her chest she would have done so.

In the afternoon when Stephen found time to phone her he found her crying.

"I'm so glad you called," she said, "I felt too weak to phone you ..."

"So you're not better?" he asked, a little annoyed.

"No, but I sent for the doctor ... I had to, as I literally couldn't get up ... and ... I couldn't contain myself ..."

"Contain yourself? What are you talking about?"

"I couldn't help it, but peed in bed ..."

"*What?!*"

"I'm sorry, but I couldn't help myself. It just happened ..."

By now it dawned upon Stephen that his wife might just be as ill as she said and that he ought to help her. It wasn't his idea of happy tidings and deep down he resented her for being this dependent upon him.

After hanging up he sat back in his chair, then he buzzed Catherine who came at once. He told her that she might have to fill in for Rosa for a week or even more as she was feeling very poorly.

Catherine's eyes glinted, her smile broadened and all her numerous charms became even more apparent. Maybe that was the first time Stephen really realized just how pretty his employee looked. Mentally he made a note of this fact and then he asked her to phone his sister-in-law, Ruth, and ask her to call him back. He had tried numerous times to himself, but in vain, and now his need for her to take over at home was so urgent that he was ready to do anything, even make a surprise-visit at her place, to do so. That was exactly what Catherine suggested, only she proposed that she went in his stead, carrying a letter from him, telling of the situation.

He agreed that that might be a good idea and after having phoned Ruth several times off she went, carrying his letter which she was to hand to her or leave at her home. Then he phoned the family doctor and asked him about the situation. It appeared that Rosa by now was so stiff in her muscles that she couldn't even turn in bed. She hadn't just had one mishap, but three or four and she was crying most of the time. All in all, the situation was chaotic as blood tests didn't tell much about the illness.

"It may be from some tick, but not one I can pinpoint for you. If she doesn't get better real soon she has to go to hospital ..."

After this phone conversation Stephen sat back, quite dumbfounded. However, what he couldn't get over was the mishaps of his otherwise so clean and fastidious wife. Rosa peeing herself – and even worse???!!! That was quite out of character. For a very long time he sat musing the situation, hoping against hope that his sister-in-law, Ruth, might suddenly appear, full of solutions to his plight.

At the same time Catherine had found out that Ruth wasn't at home. She knocked that hard on her door that her next-door-neighbor opened his door, glancing at her with suspicion and curiosity.

"Miss Lakes isn't in," the man said, "she visits her ... fiancé ..."

That was the first Catherine heard of anything like that in the life of Ruth so she looked quite bewildered at the man.

"Yes," he said, "Mr. Rogers at the second floor ... the owner of the building ..."

Catherine thanked him and then phoned Stephen to ask him what to do.

"Knock on his door and give him my letter for Charlotte ..." he suggested, very hopeful that now the helping hand he was looking for would materialize behind the door of the new boyfriend.

When Catherine knocked on the door it opened almost at once. A quite handsome and also nice-looking man appeared, obviously surprised to see her. "Are you the new pizza-delivery boy ... girl ...?" he asked.

She told him why she had come and handed him the letter. The man looked annoyed and then called to Ruth inside he flat. She appeared, scantily dressed in a man's bathrobe, but wearing a big, happy smile on a face that suddenly looked much prettier than it used to do.

When she had opened the letter and read it, she threw it on the floor and stamped her foot. "Typical!" she exclaimed. "That super egoist! How could she fall for someone like that?"

Then she pulled herself together and said, matter-of-factly: "My sister has got the flu or something like that and she needs me. Sorry, Jack, I can't stay and I don't know when I shall get back ..."

The man looked disappointed, but just hugged her and then reminded her that she was still wearing his bathrobe. Something which didn't make her blush, but only turned her a little pink in the cheeks.

On their way to see Rosa Catherine told Ruth what she knew about the situation. "I think the doctor told Mr. Carrington that she would have to go to the hospital, but that she – or he – didn't want to ..."

"That will be him," Charlotte said in an angry tone of voice, "not her. She is much too wise to fight this without help from experts."

"But it's only the flu ..."

"Hmmm – well, the flu doesn't leave one more or less paralyzed ..."

"Paralyzed?! I didn't know that ..."

Shortly after they pulled up in front of the Carrington house. Within they found chaos. The doctor was back and so was a nurse that he had called. Poor Rosa was still lying in bed, by now stiff as a board, in diapers. Her two scared eyes told about pain and terror at this situation. By now she couldn't speak anymore as the muscles in her face and throat had stiffened too.

Ruth cast one glance at her, and then she started to cry. Catherine, who didn't even like Rosa, also felt the tears trickling down her cheeks. When Ruth went over to hug her poor, prostrate sister she moaned with pain. She and Catherine decided to leave her and sat down in the sitting-room to talk to the doctor.

"We can see from blood tests that Mrs. Carrington may have been bitten by some kind of tick, but we don't know which one or how dangerous it is. Hopefully she shall recover soon, but we don't know yet what shall happen. I'm going to either leave Nurse Williams with Mrs. Carrington or have her committed to hospital. That depends on the decision of Mr. Carrington."

"To me she looks positively petrified," Charlotte said.

"Yes, and it may even be worse than it seems. She really is unable to move as much as a muscle and nobody knows what's happening to her inner organs..."

"I'm her sister," Ruth said, "and I want her committed to hospital at once."

The doctor nodded and then phoned Stephen, but he declined. He was very disappointed that Ruth didn't just go and save her sister or at least take over for him. Actually, he even thought of leaving town on some business-pretext as he simply didn't want to face either Ruth, Rosa or Catherine right now. However, he ended up going home an hour after this phone conversation because at that time the situation had changed totally: Rosa had died and Ruth was beyond herself with grief. She

17

didn't accuse him of anything, but he felt her contempt as something tangible although unspoken.

Some weeks after the funeral Ruth and her boyfriend, Jack, came to collect whatever she wanted from the belongings of her late sister. Stephen wasn't at home and although on speaking terms they hadn't met after the funeral. When Ruth dug into the vast mass of clothes, shoes, handbags and even jewels of Rosa she was nearly bitten by some strange and unknown critter. She stared at the insect and it stared back at her, the front legs lifted as if it wanted to hug her.

At first she didn't know what it could be, then it dawned upon her: This was the culprit, the murderer of her sister. She grabbed a shoe, ready to smash it when it dived into Stephen's end of the wardrobe. Here it sat, once more with lifted fore legs, and for a while they just stared at each other. Then Ruth's face turned into a mask of innocence as she slowly closed the door on the insect, careful not to crush it ...

5. When The Grim Reaper Was Killed:

Very often Sylvia crept up the big, tall tree in the backyard of her grandparents' house. When she had got high up she was almost invisible from the ground if she sat on a certain leafy branch. To the old people with their bad eyesight she was very difficult to see and, naughty as she was, she enjoyed hiding and not answering when they called her.

– Ha! she thought, they can see me, I don't believe they can't. Actually, she thought they pretended their bad eyesight, their sore muscles and joints. She simply didn't believe in the shortcomings of old age. Or rather, she wouldn't think about it as she needed them to be young and healthy for many years to come and couldn't bear losing them.

When she was a little girl of 2 years both her parents were killed in a car accident and she had been with her grandparents ever since. There was nobody else she could be with as her entire family consisted of her and those two old people, nobody else. Well, and then there was Nellie, the 14 years old golden retriever who was her very best friend. Everybody talked of Nellie as a very old dog, but Sylvia wouldn't have any of that kind of talk so she denied the truth that the dog was on her last leg.

Death was both very tangible to her and at the same time something quite imaginary. She had lost her parents to Death and accepted that it had happened, but that she herself or those she loved would die some day didn't occur to her. That's why she was so very surprised when one day she climbed the tree she found her favorite branch taken by a beautiful, little boy with angel wings.

"Hey!" she yelled. "This is my tree, in MY grandparent's backyard so beat it."

He just smiled at her, looking very friendly.

"Who are you and why are you wearing those ridiculous fake wings? You look stupid dressed like that ..."

"I do?" he said, genuinely surprised. "I put it on for you to trust me ..."

"Trust you, when you steal my tree?!"

"When I visit others I may wear other clothes ..."

"Oh, that I know. My grandparents also force me to dress differently when we go to town, the market or the doctor. When I start school I shall have to dress differently all the time."

"So you haven't started school yet, such a big girl?"

"I'm six years old and they teach me at home because I ... eh' ... get a stomach ache whenever we get near that dumb, old school."

"Smart!" he exclaimed, that I shall remember: Get a stomach ache and skip school."

Sylvia wasn't sure whether he mocked her with that comment so she glanced at him with a suspicious look. However, he looked very sincere and not at all like he intended to be fresh or anything.

"Anyway," she said, "you weren't invited to my tree so get down and don't show yourself and your ridiculous wings here again."

For a split second the lovely boy changed into something quite different and very scary, but he returned to his angel–features fast enough to make her unsure of what he had looked like for that short while.

"And who are you," she asked, all of a sudden eager to know.

"I'm Mortuus ..."

"What a ridiculous name!"

"I knew you would say that," he said, heaving a deep

sigh. "However, that's my name and if you knew it you would listen more carefully to me now."

Something in his voice really did make her listen very carefully this time and she also managed to sit still when he said: "I'm here for Nellie and your grandfather. They are to be run down by a car a few minutes from now on."

"You are the worst boy, I've ever met, and you just keep away from my Nellie and my grandfather!"

"It's my job to see to it, and what's more it will save them some of the pains of old age. It's bad enough as it is …"

Sylvia didn't want to hear one word more. She bent forward and gave the boy a hard punch in his fat angel-tummy. To her great satisfaction he tumbled down the tree and ended up motionless on the ground. Fast as a cat she climbed down and went over to him. At first she just stood staring at him, but as he didn't move she pushed him with her foot. Nothing happened and she repeated the push. When she had given him six or seven pushes he moaned and turned over to look up at her.

"That's for threatening my Nellie and my grandfather. So now you know how it is to be in an accident."

The boy looked quite bewildered, then he produced a clock from his angel's diapers and looked at it, gasping at what he saw. "Damn," he said, "now it's too late. The moment that was set for this very important and beneficent action was passed five minutes ago. Now it's too late."

"Ha!" she exclaimed, "then get up and disappear NOW!"

"What did you say right now, something about "feeling oneself how it is to be in an accident", right?"

"Yes, serves you right"

"It's true that I haven't had that experience … or the other one … before you … when you … when you pushed me …"

21

Sylvia looked at him in amazement. Was he deranged or from some weird religious sect? He looked so crazy and talked in such an idiotic way that she got quite confused.

The angel-boy sat up, rubbing his head and moaning. Then he said: "Well, it's too late for this time and the next one will not be until the stars conjoin once again which means in ... eh' ... some distant time in the future."

"You shall never set foot in this backyard again, unless you want another punch in your fat fake-angel-belly."

He just looked at her, then he bent forward and patted her head in a very tender and quite loving manner. As he did he also seemed to grow taller, his features changed from the childlike into something very old and wise. The flesh seemed to withdraw from his facial bones, his wings fell of and dissolved as they fell to the ground, and his voice changed into a deep and sonorous male voice.

Sylvia looked at him in amazement, but without being afraid.

"But dear child, I'm The Grim Reaper himself – I'm The Angel of Death."

"So that's what you are!" she yelled. "You killed my parents and you set out to murder my Nellie and my grandfather." Without uttering another word she headbuffed him so he lost his breath and staggered. Before he could regain his foothold she yelled: "Ok, Mr. Reaper-Mortuus or whatever, then don't forget that you were kicked out of this backyard. Don't return or I shall do it again!"

The Reaper stared in utter amazement at the small girl standing in front of him, this mini-Valkürie, then he burst out laughing and that was the third time she hit him, this time using her Barbie Doll. With another merry laughter he set off, up into the sky, and soon he had disappeared altogether.

6. The Stray

The sound of the alarm bell awoke me, and slowly it dawned upon me that something wasn't quite right: I wasn't lying on my bed, but on the chair. That should be impossible as the chair was narrow and only for sitting. However, there I was, and, what's more, I was coiled up upon myself in an almost uncanny way. Strange, yes, very, very strange ...

While I was contemplating the wellknown room from the chair, I suddenly saw an arm reaching out from under the duvet to turn off the alarm. I vaguely recognized it as something I knew, but not until I saw the bracelet on it. I got a shock and yelled out in terror, but without human words: "That's my arm, my bracelet in my bed, turning off my alarm clock, but I'm there. What's going on???"

From what I could see of myself, still lying on the chair, something really had changed and not for the better.Yes, that's for sure, because what I saw when I scanned my entire frame was the shiny fur of a black cat. This being such a crazy situation at first I refused to accept it as part of the everyday reality that was mine, but shrugged it off as a nightmare. However, when I in my cat's shape saw myself—Rosie Kingston—sitting up on my bed in my human shape, smiling upon me, the cat, I got mad as Hell.

With a sound like 10 stray cats and at least one lion I bounced upon the woman on the bed, who somehow had stolen my identity. Yes, who had become Rosie who in reality was me.

The woman screamed, but she also fought back and at one point she got a fierce blow in that sent me flying.

"The sedative," she yelled, "Rainier, she is awake ..."

While I was trying to recuperate I saw a pair of naked, hairy men's legs beside the woman's legs and I recognized Rainier who actually was my husband although he behaved like he was married to my "identical twin" on the bed.

With a less than friendly smile he proceeded to produce a syringe and emptied it into my nice, soft and furry, black cat buttocks. Soon after I fell asleep once again, but at that moment I knew that my last impression of the two people and the blood on the bed sheets from my attack on the woman would stay with me forever. I knew that for sure as I dropped off into dreamland ...

When I awoke once again I soon saw that now I was confined to the cat's transport cage. Rainier was sitting on the chair where I awoke some minutes (or maybe hours?) before.

He still held the syringe in his hands.

"Hello," he said, "so you're with us once again? How nice ..." The last words were charged with irony and I knew him well enough to see that he really felt like plunging the needle of the syringe right into me once more.

"I know that this is confusing to you, my dear, but with a little patience you'll get through these weeks like the rest of us ..."

All I could do was to purr, meow, scream and sort of splutter sounds that scared even me. However, sitting in the cage I knew that I had to cooperate to get out again. That's the reason why I smiled at him, but that only infuriatds him and he yelled: "What, are you threatening me too? Don't my dear, or off we march to the vet ... However, as I can see you understand me I shall tell you what's going on. Well, you and our former pet cat, Mitzi, have exchanged bodies, and I can assure you that Mitzi is a very, very successful "you". She knows exactly what I want from her, and she is quite bright—almost a genius—when it comes to computers."

I couldn't help myself, but let out a plaintive "meow" at this eulogy. So Mitzi, my pet cat, had replaced me in my own home, had virtually stolen my life? Unbelievable, but the evidence couldn't be denied.

When the door opened and the former Mitzi, now Mrs. Rosie Kingston, stepped into the room I uttered a deep felt hiss. Oh, how I would have loved to scratch those long legs that in reality belonged to me, but which she, the cat, had stolen from me.

"Hello cutie," she said, "oh, how it becomes you to sit in a cage. It goes so very well with your claws and fangs."

I could have killed her over the irony of that remark. How dared she to taunt me? She was nothing but a stray picked off the road when she was starving and now she was loading it over me, her mistress! Too much, much, much too much ...

She kicked the cage one big, brutal kick, and quite enough to frighten me as I sat there without any chances of escape. "All right," she said, "and now you're wondering at how I—well, we—did it. To know the internet is to know a lot of websites with special information, also about magic, so that's what I've been browsing as I'm not being such a stupid cow—eh', cat—as you ..."

My head was spinning with surprise. The internet? Well, yes, as a cat she had always been very interested in games on the computer and that kind of stuff. When my computer was on she used to sit in front of it and sometimes I caught her sitting right on the keyboard so, crazy as it sounds, still it did make some kind of sense.

"Also I suppose that you would like to know when we shall take you to the vet to have you put down, right?"

I must admit that that was an urgent question with me so I stared at her, following each movement.

"Well, we can't yet as the transference of your body to mine must be complete before we do anything about it and that takes some time. Besides, that part of it is Rainier's responsibility, not mine."

With that piece of information she left as there was somebody at the door. Rainier came into the room and he took on from where she left: "Yes, that will be the day," he said, "at long last to get rid of you is my dream!"

I wanted to ask him why he hated me that much, but I already knew the answer: My recent love affair with John Hansson had made him furious and he would never forgive me for being unfaithful.

"Mitzi is my dream girl," he said.

"Yes," I said in cat's language, but are you her dream man?" That I simply didn't believe from the way she talked of him. As I said so, both of us heard a shuffle and a muffled shout at the door. Then a shot rang out which made Rainier look absolutely terrified. When the door was flung open and a wild-eyed, young man stood there, ready to shoot once more I wasn't all that surprised. It was John Hansson and he was beyond himself with rage.

Behind him stood a bloodied and still bleeding Mitzi. She too looked terrified, but she also started to beg John and Rainier call the police and an ambulance. John's reply was to raise the gun and shoot her in the head. As she fell to the floor Rainier shot up, either to flee or to fight, I didn't know which. Once more John raised the gun and shot him too, then he even aimed at me, the cat, but relented and put the weapon against himself.

There I was, sitting in a cage, surrounded by three dead people. Luckily enough the shootings had been overheard and soon after the police came and with them also the animal welfare-people who took me into custody. I was with them less than a week before I was adopted by a pretty and even famous, young woman who actually leads a wonderful life as a model. As it is she always lets her computer run, doesn't ever turn it off, and what's more, she never-ever puts me in the cage. No, with her a cat can roam, even sit on the keyboard, browsing whatever there is to browse, like e.g. something about magic and new beginnings in life ...

7. Nightmares:

Once there was a sleepy man called Timmy, always digging deep into sleep. Sometimes he endured hardships of various kinds, but then he just went to sleep and dreamt. The dreams cleared his mind and then he didn't care about all the evilness in his life. However, one day his little daughter asked him a question: "Why do you always lose your job, Daddy. Your clothes get ruined and someone steals your money, but why does these things always happen to you?" That question he couldn't dream away, he thought it over and then he said: "I don't know, but everyone meets hardships in their life. It doesn't matter. It stops again."

His daughter looked at him with the skepticism of an eight year old girl. "Hmmm," she said. "I don't like that, I want to have fun always ..."

He tried to convince her that although some bad things happened to some people, it didn't matter that much when one had the right attitude. No matter what, he couldn't get through to her so he was sad that night when he went to sleep. Perhaps that's why he had an awful nightmare. Some shadowy creatures came to him as he lay there in his nice, warm bed. They poked at him and one said in a voice full of contempt: "So you endure everything, and don't fear us?"

"Fear you?" he exclaimed, very surprised.

"Yes, you idiot, didn't you know that your bad luck came from somewhere?"

He was shaken to the core of his being. "Some people do encounter bad luck, but there is nothing one can do about it ..."

"He, he, he," the creature went on in a horse and contemptuous voice. "No, if one doesn't do anything then there is nothing to be done."

He was stopped by another of the black shadowy things, waving a long and very thin arm at him. "All right, the contemptuous one said, "dream your dreams and have fun in your misery."

"Nice meeting you," another one said with a grin that bared pointed, white teeth. "Very nice indeed, you are so special compared to what we are used to ..."

"But what is all this, am I hexed or what is going on?" No answer, but the shadowy ones dissolved with a crackling laughter and he woke up, utterly uncomfortable. However, after a couple of hours tossing on his bed he fell asleep once again and this time he had another kind of dream. He saw one of the shadowy ones come running against him, spear in hand and before he could do anything about it he pierced his chest, right through the heart. Once more he woke up, feeling miserable, almost expecting to find marks after the spear. "What is going on?" he asked in a loud voice into the darkness of his bedroom.

"Nothing," a voice rung out from the darkness and he nearly tumbled down from his bed with fright at this unexpected answer. "Nothing at all, so you better just sleep on."

He sat up in his bed, ready to jump out and then he turned on the light with trembling fingers. There was nothing to be seen, but the voice from before still sounded out in the room. "We are very sorry that our younger soldiers came to disclose their presence. The clients are not supposed to know about us."

"The clients!" he exclaimed, "that is a mistake, I'm no client. I'm a private investigator and I have clients ...."

"You sure do," the voice said. "One of them remembers you uncommonly well. He may never forget you."

29

"And who may that be?"

"Alfie Johnson, the man whose daughter disappeared and he committed suicide over this unhappy incident ..."

"Oh yes," he said, "I remember that case. And she never came back?"

"We know where she is, but you were supposed to find her, instead you did a lot of other things that amused you more than that."

"And is that why I have all this bad luck? I don't believe in bad luck, only that some events are less than good."

"Some people are vengeful, you're not, you want to forgive everything even before it happens."

"But Alfie ... well, suffice it to say that he doesn't forget that he has lost his daughter and also his life because of you."

"Am I to believe that Alfie Johnson has harmed me, that he is behind all this?" He couldn't help laughing at the thought, but that made the voice turn harsher as it said: "Poor Timmy, Alfie Johnson is with you all the time, no matter what, he is always close by."

Timmy laughed once more: "What!" he exclaimed, "Where are you? I can't see you, this is just a dream and I'm talking to myself."

"So this is another one of your dreams, nothing real ever happens to you, does it?" it sounded from somewhere else in the room.

Suddenly the door opened and his daughter came in. "Daddy, why do you shout like that, it's the night, you should sleep." He left the bed and followed her into her room, tucked her in her bed, adding some consolatory words. "Don't be afraid, Daddy is just having some bad dreams ..."

She looked at him with love and doubt intermingled, the very picture of her late mother, but she didn't seem convinced.

"A nice daughter you have," the voice said when he returned into his bedroom. "Very sweet, resembles Alfie's little Isabel when she was her age."

"Back off!" he yelled, suddenly alarmed, "just you dare and I shall rip you apart."

"He, he, he, he," it sounded from the darkness, "and how will you go about that when you can't even see us?" He laughed out once more and then there was quiet.

Timmy called out for the one who had shouted at him, but got no answer. Then he went to bed and at once started to dream again. This time the shadowy ones were standing very close by his bed, he could see them, but they were totally silent, until a sugary voice asked: "What is the name of your pretty daughter?"

The question seemed so sinister to him that he felt chills running up and down his spine.

"Yes, what's her name?" asked another one and soon all of them asked the same question: "The name? The name?" Timmy felt how this question went deep down his heart, and he simply lost his conscience from fright.

However, when he came to himself some time after, he saw the sunlight and felt a deep relief. – Oh, thank God, that too was only a dream. All of it dreams, not Alfie, no shadows or spears. No questions ..., he thought.

Exactly at the same moment when this thought passed through his head his daughter stood by his bed, looking at him with a worried look. "Are you sick, Daddy?" she asked.

"No, dear, Daddy only has had several nightmares ..." he answered.

She looked at him in astonishment. "But you didn't sleep," she said, "you were so busy walking around and moving things ..."

"What?!" he exclaimed in amazement. "No, I slept and had many bad dreams about things that don't exist."

31

"You pulled down the curtains and you ruined some plates in the kitchen ..."

"No, no, I slept most of the night although I had nightmares."

Her look made him get out of bed and he followed her, convinced that this must be a mistake. However, when he opened the door into the kitchen he found havoc. "What, is this?" he exclaimed, utterly amazed.

"You did it," the little girl said, "you also pulled down the curtains and ripped them."

"No! I slept, I dreamt ... It wasn't real ..." – ""It wasn't real"" resounded and he suddenly remembered the shadowy one's remark: "So this is another one of your dreams, nothing real ever happens to you, does it?"

She didn't say anything, only looked worried at him. "The only time I was up was when I tucked you in after you came to see me ..."

"What? No, you didn't do that," his daughter said, "the man did ..."

"The man??!"

"Yes, your friend Alfie ... He said you were asleep although you were not. A very nice man, asked my name and patted my head ..."

8. Cats, Rats and Poison

Sometimes it pays off to have a chat with one's dinner. Yes, it sure does, especially if you're a cat about to set your teeth into a poisoned mouse. This time it was Greg the mouse about to be eaten by Beauty, the cat. At the exact moment her teeth were lowered and were just about to sink into Greg he said:

"Eh', excuse me, but that's not good for you, Madam Cat."

Never before had Beauty's dinner talked to her except by excessive curses or prayers for mercy so she was very, very surprised when this happened. Also by the polite tone in this small, but tasty treat. She looked at him in amazement when he once more spoke:

"Yes, I'm dangerous to eat because I had the misfortune to eat some rat poison the other day."

"Rat poison?" Beauty exclaimed. "If you had eaten rat poison you would have been dead by now."

"I don't feel all too well so I'm sure to die soon, maybe in a few minutes. However, I shall still be a lethal meal, even for you, Madam Cat."

"What nonsense is this?" Beauty exclaimed, "It can't have been rat poison ..."

"All the others died," Greg said, wiping his eyes with his tail. "Oh, so very sad, you would not want to experience anything like that. Especially not when you have such bright and pretty young ones to look after ..."

"What do you know about my children? How did you know that they are pretty and bright?"

"I'm sure they take after you, Madam Cat," Greg said with a sneaky look on his face.

Like all cats Beauty always succumbed very easily to flattery. If somebody told her that she was pretty she looooved that individual. Still, the sly expression on the small mousy face made her distrust him. – He is a master of flattery, she thought to herself, and I bet he is a liar too.

"You, sir, lie," she said, looking at him with a stern glance, "you don't want to be eaten and that's the truth." Having said this she – oh horror of horrors – ate him, tail, ears, whiskers and the rest in one gulp. After having done this she at once started to feel a little worried because didn't her stomach behave in a strange way? Maybe he had been right so that now she was poisoned? She lay down feeling a bit nauseated. Yes, she felt so worried and insecure of herself and her own judgment that she didn't hear the not all that soft patters of paws behind her until she felt the teeth of the Jones–family's dog, Tarzan, in her neck.

"Help!" she screamed, but nobody came to her rescue. Instead Tarzan began to laugh.

"You stupid and ugly cat, you homeless bag of fleas, that's for lying down and not being alert to dogs."

"I had to lie down," she yelled, "I'm sick!"

"Sick? Ha! I don't believe you."

"I've eaten Greg the Mouse even though he was contaminated by rat poison."

"Oh, my God!" Tarzan exclaimed. "That's awful." He let go of her neck, but pinned her down with one of his large paws.

"Yeeees," she whined, "and I feel so sick. Everything is getting black right before my eyes and I'm dizzy ..."

"Not good, no, not good, especially as you're a mother of young ones. Maybe I better snap your neck to bring you out of your misery ...."

"What?!!! No, no, and besides, that would contaminate your teeth – it may already have happened – so that you too die."

"Hmmmm," he said, "you may have a point there, but I never bit you to bleed so I'm all right."

"Do you mind removing your paw from my back, it makes me even more nauseated to be pinned down like that?"

"If I did you would run and that wouldn't be right to either you or the little ones now that I know you're poisonous. Your milk would kill them and you would suffer a most awful death so I really shall have to snap your neck ..."

"Help!Help!" Beauty wailed and this time someone came running. It turned out to be the owner of Tarzan who grabbed him by his collar and lifted him off her.

"Oh no, you poor, homeless thing," he said letting go of Tarzan and lifting Beauty up into his protective arms. Tarzan was very upset at this development in the drama, especially as he soon afterwards could see Beauty and her boisterous brood sitting in HIS sitting-room with HIS human being and eating HIS food while she was being petted by everyone in HIS house. She looked fit as a fiddle and whenever anybody mentioned Greg to her in the days to come she said, full of disgust:

"What a liar! He hadn't eaten poison at all, only wanted to scare me. I'm glad I ate him."

As to Tarzan then he was beyond himself with regret that he hadn't eaten the damn cat, the criminal, lying mothball, who took over HIS family, HIS house and HIS favorite sleeping place: The lap of his beloved Master.

9. Angel

I was awoken in the darkest of nights, the air was ablaze with sounds. Something like cracks of whips made waves and I turned ice. "No one whips my air," I said, brazing myself, "or else ..."

"Sorry," it came from the darkness.

I didn't turn on the light, but now I saw the outline of her intruder. It was the Angel of Whatever, who seemed to consist of whirrs of sounds and wings. "Don't be alarmed. I come with a message"

"What?! No," I said, "no messages. I'm not Mary."

The whippings of air and all the sounds stopped at once. "Not Mary? How come?"

"Not all women are Mary, by God!"

"They are not? How strange, The Big Guy seems to think so."

"I believe you, actually, it's obvious that contrary to common belief he doesn't know everything."

The air froze, the whirrs exploded in fastness so that they too blended and froze into one movement. "That's sacrilege ..." he stuttered.

"Yeah, yeah," I said, "now leave me so I can get some sleep."

"I can't leave you after what you said, now I shall have to stay forever." Having said so he started another barrage of whirrs. Sounds and whippings went crazy and I let out an involuntary high pitched scream. "Stop it! Go away, and don't come back!"

He lifted from the floor and sailed through the air, a big, not too agile airship–like creature, an angel, targeting me for conversion. "My God, you're stubborn!" I exclaimed. "And this ... this chaos is supposed to converse me?"

He looked very surprised at me. "Chaos? This is not chaos, it's anything but chaos."

"Well," I said, now sitting up in my bed, very annoyed, "and what do you want with me?"

"It's that message ... You are supposed to give birth to his daughter and to save the world."

"What!!!!!" I sputtered, crimson-red in the face. "How ... how ... daughter ... Earth. I distinctly remember what happened to his son ..."

"The Highest One of the Highest said so himself, you are to find a way to save the world and make everything better. What son are you talking about, he doesn't have one?"

"Doesn't have one? Well, that's what I've always said, but never mind. If he wants me then why did he make me an ordinary woman, and not even rich or very healthy? Not to speak of younger?"

The angel kept silent, looking very petulant, but also deep in thoughts. "Well, I can't tell you why he chose you, but he did. He has high hopes of you."

"And what am I to gain by that scheme?"

"Gain?!!Eternal happiness as the one who saved the world!!!"

"Aha – something I gain after Death?"

"Yes, don't you know that "save" also means" "sacrifice" ...?

"Sacrifice like in Crucifixion? Sorry to have to inform you that I just turned down the job. Give him my love and tell him to find someone else."

"No-no-no, that wouldn't do. It's you or nobody. You are to stop the ..."

"I'm a widowed and childless housewife and salesperson," I don't know anything about saving anything by giving birth ..." By now I was getting a bit angry and, for some reason or another, not being afraid of this creature I turned on the lamp by my bed. Suddenly the angel was visible to the sight – and that was the moment I started to SCREAM: An angel yes, but coal-black, red goat-eyes, claws for hands and a pointed tail. His wings were very large, black and rubber-like.

When I screamed in utter disgust and horror one of his claws shot out and clamped my mouth shut. "Now-now," he said, "nothing to fret about, he likes you a lot and he is sure you are going to fit in just fine. After having read your biography – stealing, eh'? fraud? even murder, eh'? – I'm convinced you'll like it too ..." Then he grabbed me and lifted me up in one single movement and off we flew ...

10. Walls and Floors

The lion said something and everyone at the animal-congress listened. What he said was "dinner". All the animals pricked up their ears and most of them moved a little further back from him, except those very stupid and young ones who hadn't heard of his eating habits. The rest edged off to one side away from him. However, the crocodile who himself was often thinking about dinner wasn't afraid of this old and sick fur-ball, but went up to him and said: "Is that so and where is it?"

"You misunderstand me," the lion went on, "we are not having dinner here or now, but what I want to know is why those men shot at me four times."

"Four times!" The leopard yelled. "Me they shot at many more times, but me they didn't hit. I was too fast for them ..."

Everyone looked askance at the wounds on the lion's back and some even smiled a little to him- or herself. He noticed it and made a mental list of all those little smug smiles. – Just you wait, he thought, but he didn't say anything.

"And all your wives and children were shot too ..." the leopard went on, obviously gloating at the thought.

"Ok, ok, very sad and all that," the crocodile said, "but what about the dinner?"

The lion heaved a sigh and said: "That's the crazy part of it, they shot my entire family, but I've never heard of people eating lions ..."

"Oh, I see," the vulture said, "you wonder at this massacre when lion's meat isn't high on the menu of the humans. Not that I haven't ... well, the taste in meat of predators – which you are – is somewhat different from what we find in those who don't eat all that meat ... not that I mind it ..." One fierce look from the lion who suspected that the dead bodies of his five wives and all his children might have been on his and his friends' menu made him shut up.

The zebra who had relatives who had been shot by the same men ventured an answer to the lion: "When my Mom, my uncle and two of my cousins were shot I heard the murderers talk of something called "walls" and "floors"."

"Yes!" the leopard yelled, "me too when they shot at me – but without hitting me – the foreign huntsman mentioned something about it, but the native ones didn't just go for that. They would sell some parts of us and in that way get "money" – whatever that is – to get food and a lot of other things. But they didn't intend to eat us ..."

"So they murder us for something called "walls" and "floors", and sell parts of us ... to me that sounds sick," the wart hog said, looking very glum.

"Not you," the little naughty monkey yelled. "You're much too ugly to be shot for floors and walls, but they might eat you."

The wart hog snorted in contempt at this little, naughty one who had been away from their habitat for the most of her life, but then suddenly had reappeared among them. Many rumors told of imprisonment for thieving and assaults, but nobody really knew what had happened. That's why all of them pricked up their ears when she went on:

"I've heard that you think I've been to jail for naughtiness until recently. In a way it's true, but not altogether."

"I knew it," the wart hog said, triumphantly. She didn't like the monkey who often teased her and her children. Now that she – who was considered a beauty among her own – had been called "ugly" by her she positively hated her.

"Well, I was stolen from my Mom, whom they shot dead when I was quite tiny," the monkey said, looking very sad. "Then they took me to something called "England" and made a pet out of me. It wasn't a bad life as such when I was a baby, but when I grew up to become a beauty I, of course, wanted someone to appreciate my looks and that meant that I clamored for male attention .... I wanted to have my own family of beautiful monkey babies ...."

"Beautiful babies?!" the wart hog snorted, "nothing as ugly as those creatures with hands all over ...."

"Better than hooves, or whatever it is you have," the monkey said.

"Well, where does all this lead?" the lion said, quite annoyed. "Were your Mom their dinner, or why did they shoot her?"

"To get hold of me."

"I don't understand anything of this," the lion went on. "They shoot your Mom, grabbed you for England and now you're back ..."

"Yes, when my old master died his daughter inherited me and the castle we lived in. The castle she kept, but me she got rid of. According to what she said she found that I deserved to see my own kind and to go back to live among them. Not that I blame her, but had she found a husband for me I might have preferred to stay in England and be pampered by her or her children."

"Hmmmmm," the zebra said, "a strange tale, but you said something about knowing "walls" and "floors" ..."

"Yes, they have an idea of homes being like a whole line of connected caves. With us at the castle each cave had a name and in a couple of them I found relatives of some of you. For instance, there was a zebra on the floor of the study ...."

"What do you mean?" the zebra yelled."A zebra on the floor?!!!"

"OK, not an entire zebra, but the skin was spread out on the floor for these humans to step on."

"Perversion!" the zebra cried, beyond himself with disgust. "Do you mean to tell me that my relatives died for their skins to be trod on?"

"Yes, but there also was one on the wall. As to the lion in the castle ...."

"Was there a lion? How did it look and what did it do?" The lion asked.

"Do? Not much as it was stuffed ..."

"Stuffed??? Whatever do you mean?"

"They take out the organs inside the lion and do something to the skin which they then stuff with some special material. That makes the body look quite alive, but it's dead."

"Why did they do something that horrible?" the antelope said. He was quite shaken by this news.

"Well, they do it to your people too. Also to zebras and other animals."

"Not to us!" the rhinoceros yelled.

"Oh yes, you too. However, only the lions and some of the others go on the walls. Here they are put up as adornments – or parts of them are ....."

"Parts of us?" The lion looked quite bewildered once again.

"Your head, your paws or maybe just your skin."

"Perversions!" the leopard whispered, looking very disgusted.

The monkey turned to face him and then she said: "With you it's much more than just head and paws. You see, the ladies – that is the human she-ones – love the pattern of your skin and although it's not allowed anymore the hunt is for skins they can make clothes from."

"That can't be," the leopard said. "How would they make clothes from my skin?"

"They do and they call it a fur-coat. It's very expensive
– never mind that, I can't explain that word right now as
I have to be back before sunset – but they strip the dead
leopard of its skin for coats, the head and maybe also the
paws go on the wall."

All the animals looked at each other in disgust. "What
perverts these humans are," the lion said. "Next time I
come across some I shall eat them right away."

"Yeah-yeah," all the animals said, looking quite fierce
and also determined to have it done. "They don't deserve
better."

"No," the lion said, "and because they killed my beautiful
family for paws and heads and skins I shall find it difficult
to remarry. Fewer and fewer of us, more and more of
them. They are like an illness spreading everywhere ..."

The animals sighed. All of them did just that and soon
after they went along on each their way because the
sunset was close at hand and they knew that the wounded
lion might forget that they were neither dinner nor snack
for him, but participants in the animal-congress.

– Eat and be eaten, the vulture thought, but floors and
walls, that's too much. He set off from his branch and flew
out to the carcass of one of the lion's pups who had died
that same day from his wounds after the shooting.

11. Floating

This wasn't the best way to start the day. Everything went on in slowmotion and I couldn't make myself move. I just lay there, stuck, flat on my back even when trailing my arms and legs over the white sheets of the bed. The sharp, metallic sounds from nowhere and everywhere blended in with the wallpaper quality of anonymity in this room that wasn't mine, not even my choice. I was brought here and vaguely remembered when they lifted me off the pavement and put me on the stretcher. "Careful, careful," someone yelled, perhaps the one who had called 911, when he found me, "poor creature, looks like a stroke."

Yeah, I thought, more like a blow to my head. More like something–out–of–nowhere that made my head spin, my legs fold, and my soul slither down my spine, untying each chakra as it went. When I fell, I was dead, and when someone grabbed my purse and kicked me in the stomach before running off the pain brought me back to the bleak realities of being robbed and not being able to move.

I suppose I should be grateful for that revival, but somehow I couldn't. When those two came to visit me, lying there, I even regretted having collected my chakras and returned back to life.

So those people were my close relatives? The one in black and purple looked nightmarish, like a vampire, and she even kissed me and called me "My dear". The other one, so stiff in the features that they almost creaked when they moved with something that vaguely resembled a smile, called me "Mom". I was appalled. This creaky one came from ME? Then what was – or am – I to have produced anything like that robotic creature?

The thought made me spin in my white room with all the instruments, the syringes by the bed, and the nurses whipping in and out the door. How did that happen in my world of wavering colors, sounds like deep sea murmurings and floating in and out of flowery realms? Not me, no, not the one without any anchors in the world of necessity. All that was left on that pavement and now brought back as a rerun of old movies, something in black and white that's so very much in the past that it feels quite creepy as all the actors are gone long ago.

Still, that stiff face did hurt, only I didn't know why.

They talked of chances, life expectancies, of treatments, hopelessness and of insurances. The discussion even got heated, stiff-face cracked and the word "money" escaped those thin, thin lips, but black–and–purple said "hope". I knew that meant new syringes, new treatments and new floatings somewhere out of their reach and into that world of colors and sounds, anchored by the presumed wish to stop floating. As if ....

12. Blending In

When she came to the park she started to walk toward the lake. She could glimpse it in between the trees as she glanced down the sloping lawn. – What a beautiful place, she thought to herself. And all those birds ... She looked up into the sky and saw them, her wonderful, small darlings, seemingly heading for the lake, just as she was. The sight made her smile to herself and without thinking about it she fingered the big bag with bread that she was clutching.

She loved to see the birds, but she also enjoyed watching all the beautiful flowers. – A very good gardener here, she thought to herself and nodded at the thought, wonder who he is. Some beds of tulips in all colors stood out against the green of the grass and the trees. This sight made her stop some minutes, breathing in all this beauty and she felt how it filled her and made her a part of it. No limits, no borders, all of it was beauty.

At the exact same moment the thought of being part of this beautiful world filled her and she felt so elevated by this feeling. Some young people passed by on the pathway. She didn't turn to look at them, but caught their laughter and some words out of context. All of it, both the laughter, the words and the fast movements collided with her own wonderful feelings. The words "Strange ...", "ridiculous...", "look, what is THAT? ..." came right at her and then there was another bout of laughter ...

– Oh no, she thought, starting her usual appeal to God. However, then she realized that they had gone and at once she hurried toward the lake.

– What a lot of darlings today, she thought to herself when she saw them, both on the shore and in the water.

Perhaps they knew I was coming. The idea was pleasing to her, she loved to think that these pretty creatures knew her and needed her, yes, that she meant something to them.

At the lake she started to feed them bread from her bag. Bread, cut into small cubicles, bird's seed and some cookies she had left for them, everything was for her darlings.

After having fed them for a while she sat down at the bench by the lake that she called "her place". Nobody came there, but she found it perfect, no prying eyes and also tactical for bird feeding. When she had fed them the bulk of her bag, but somehow not the cookies. She sat back and right away her hand found the cookies she had brought for the birds and lifted them to her mouth. She was a bit ashamed of eating what she had intended to give the birds, but on the other hand, wasn't she tired after the walk in the park? Wasn't hunger a normal reaction? Yes to both, it was all very normal, she thought.

Sitting there on the sunlit bench, cookies in her hand and in her mouth, birds chirping and everything being so pretty, she let herself sink into the light and the beauty of it all. She felt how the scenery filled her and made her happy to be part of it, as if it had a special room prepared for her and this bench by the lake was the center of it.

However, she also felt quite drowsy. That is, suddenly she realized that what she felt was her own suddenly so small and insignificant frame blending in with all this beauty and peace. The thought lifted her very soul and there was happiness in every atom of her being, however, almost at that same moment she heard the noisy young people once again. The laughter rippled through the stillness and before long there they were, a few meters from her.

She heard them talk to themselves, and then suddenly a shrill boy's voice rang out: "How disgusting! A circus tent all by itself ... or is it an elephant?"

"No, Duckie, it's a hippo ... the disgusting fatso ..."

She knew they were talking about her, that they wanted to make her angry, but somehow she didn't understand what they said. "Circus tent?""Hippo?"

"How ugly it is, that creature of the lake," the pretty, young girl said, "shouldn't be let out of its cage." Then they laughed and moved on, past her as she was sitting there in the blessed sunlight, suddenly blotting it out as they passed her. The shadow that came from their perfect, young bodies encompassed her for a short moment, then they were gone, still laughing ...

She sat dumbfounded, both sad and in shock, but first and foremost surprised. – What have I done to them? Why do they do this to me? she thought.

The shadow was gone when they left, but somehow it was as if it was still lingering and it made her shudder, suddenly freezing sitting there, alone in the sunlight, ...

13. The Day Face

Brenda really liked Stanley, even when she killed him. Her hands, sometimes quite unwilling instruments, snapped his neck in seconds after his hands came to rest on what she herself called "the line". No one passed that line, and no one found it and lived, even though she might like them both before and after doing what she had to do.

Stanley fell to the ground like a ragdoll and she passed his sprawled dead body in one step. Something which only very long legs make possible and thus something that came natural to her, being tall and statuesque. After passing his dead body she simply went home and started her night ceremony, even before eating. Actually, she didn't feel like eating anything this evening and she really felt bereaved by the death of poor Stanley whom she had come to like over the past two weeks. She felt that for once she understood a man – and then he had to go like that.

Heaving a deep sigh she started the intricate process of removing her day face. She knew that having done so she would feel a little better without all the make-up that she felt obliged to use. Not that she liked it, but what has to be done has to be done and the make-up was a must ...

Working on her face one more sigh escaped her when she came to think of the others who had been too close to that special line. Some were just brushed off before anything happened and others had ended up like poor Stanley.

One of them had been Rick who thought that she had been playful when she pulled back from him. He too had had his hands on that special line while tracing her amazing beauty. "Aha," he said, "so you had one of those, those, what do you call them, beauty surgeries ..." He laughed out loudly and then kissed her forehead lovingly. "Well, the result is stunning, darling, and you don't have to tell me about it. I love you as you are, scars and all."

She knew he did and so did Peter, the first of her admirers who definitely had had to go. In his case there was absolutely no other solution as he not only found the line, but crossed it. Suddenly, and quite unexpectedly on her part as she had been assured over and over again that it couldn't happen, what was hidden was revealed. He had started to scream and that was when she learnt the use of the technique of snapping necks in seconds.

Now, this evening, she felt sad at thinking of those who had died, but being practical she sent the message of Stanley's death to Emperor. His face at once appeared on the screen that was concealed in her mirror. She just said one word and he nodded: "Dead."

"Remove."

Once more he nodded and then he opened his mouth as if he wanted to tell her something, but she brushed him off. "Not to-night, Emperor. I'm tired and want to go to sleep."

"OK," he said, "I shall see to everything. Sleep tight and don't worry about this." His handsome and familiar face dissolved into fragments of green and he was gone.

At the same time Brenda's hands went to the line. One forefinger hooked on the loop, she pulled it and in second her mirror showed her the image she liked the best: The green lizard-face of the so-called alien from her far-away home-planet.

Happy once again she traced her features and felt reassured at finding herself once again now that her artificial, human day-face was off. Now that it stared back at her from its box she felt a deep relief that it wasn't really hers ....

14. A Hospital of Sorts

Evelyn felt a strong relief at the sight that met her after her surgery. Everywhere around her bed tall, efficient-looking white figures were swarming.

OK, she was still not feeling quite well after the accident, but now she was in the hands of capable people who seemed eager to look after her. - That's all right, she thought to herself, I shall get well and return to my job and my family. Thinking this she suddenly realized that she was thinking first of her job and secondly of her family. That was what she had often been accused of by her husband Charles and now she noticed it herself.

- Yes, yes, she told herself, I'm baaaad, but then I have a job and even a career which poor old Charles hasn't.

One of the white figures came up to her bed at the exact moment she had this thought. He - or was it a she, it was quite difficult to see because their uni-sex uniform was so special - looked into her face and flashed a gentle smile at her, but he/she didn't speak.

Evelyn felt like talking so she said: "When do you think I shall get out of here?"

The nurse - or whatever this person was - smiled once more and then said: "You shouldn't think too much, but just rest and regain your strength." Then he/she patted her good, but rather limp hand and turned away.

That made Evelyn look at the poor, injured hand which strangely enough didn't hurt anymore. She shouted in a cheerful voice: "I'm glad to report that the pain has gone away."

The nurse turned around and looked at her with a puzzled look, then he/she smiled once more: "Of course and now you should rest a while and maybe get out of bed later this afternoon."

In the afternoon another person in white came to see her. He/she helped her out of bed and suggested that they took a short walk down the hall. Evelyn didn't feel like it, but then decided to comply as she really wanted to get well and start working again.

Off they went down what seemed to be an endless hall. Far ahead of them there was another small group of patients with nurses, but somehow they soon caught up with them.

This group consisted of three young patients with two nurses and Evelyn soon got quite friendly with the two girls. As to the young man then he seemed exceedingly angry or bitter at something so she kept her distance. – Wonder what's eating him, she thought to herself, but she didn't like to ask the others although she heard that they had been in the same accident..

The girls were 18 and 20 years old and they were giggly and cheerful. Evelyn wondered at their cheerfulness as they obviously were more severely hurt than the man. She couldn't help commenting on this to the eldest of them, Shirley: "How come that you and your friend are so cheerful and happy although both of you have lost a leg in that car accident?"

"Oh, that's easy," she said, "we don't need it here. Actually we don't need it anymore."

"What do you mean?" Evelyn said. "To be without a leg is burdensome and may also give you social problems."

Shirley just looked at her and then her friend, Eve, said: "Not here, all that is over."

Evelyn was so surprised at this attitude which also indicated that they thought they were to stay in hospital all their lives. She saw to it that she came to walk by herself with Shirley and then she said: "But you are going to be discharged and then you return to your ordinary life ..."

This time Shirley just stared at her and she felt that she had been rude in talking about her private life and health. Soon after they left as Evelyn wanted to go back to her bed and rest a little. However, her nurse suggested that they went to see some of the patients who never had any visitors. Annoyed, but eager to show her benevolent spirit she accepted the suggestion and off they went into a ward swarming with white figures.

"Do you remember that you were here?" her nurse asked her. "That your former bed is by the window?"

"No, that can't be, I only hurt my hand. All these patients look much more sick."

"Mmmm," the nurse said, "and so were you, but now you're getting so much better minute by minute."

"Yes, the doctors here work miracles. I'm very grateful for what they have done to help me."

Exactly at that moment something special happened: A door opened and a flock of white figures came into the room. They went straight up to four beds and started to wheel them out the room. At the same time some others brought new patients, already in bed as they all seemed to be in a coma.

"Do you remember it now?" the nurse said.

"Not really," Evelyn answered. "No, actually not at all."

"Strange," the nurse said, "because you were such an easy patient: From coma to --- well, and now up and walking ..."

"Yes, you are amazing here," she answered, feeling genuine admiration. "However, I would like to know when I may return back to work ..."

"My dear lady, you don't understand this situation." Suddenly looking a bit annoyed at this dimness in her he/ she made a very fast movement. The uniform that all of them wore sort of fell apart and turned into two large, white wings.

Evelyn screamed when she saw them being unfolded thus turning the nurse into something much more specialized.

"I'm sorry, he/she said, but you are one of the very few who don't understand the situation when they come here."

"Are you telling me that I'm ... that I'm dying?"

"My dear Evelyn what can I say and what did you expect of me?"

"To be cured! To return back to my life!" Her voice grew shrill and it broke several times before it was quenched in tears.

"Oh dear," the white one said, "that's all over as your body has gone, so to speak. However, don't be so sad. I'm sure you shall like it up here."

Blended with tears she didn't answer, but only turned on her heel and started to look for her bed. He/she didn't follow her, but stayed in the same spot, watching as she left, suddenly staggering with her shock.

II Poems

1. Ophelia

I'm Ophelia
allow me to drown
in water one's heart floats so well
lovely to get it washed
to free it of royal love images
stale to the touch

After all, nothing like reapers
no princes kisses like him
yes, grimness holds a certain charm
cold skeleton hands hug the best

2. The Desire

In the center
desire
all of it turned into hungry lips
hunger
thirst

3. Desire

The sucking?
Much like a rosy piston
blooming in pleasure

Plural mouths alive with desire
none of them satiated
giving and taking alike

4. In the Morning

In the morning
make like a tree
stand tall
be productive
grow roots
sprout branches
make room for birds

In the evening
uproot yourself
spread your wings
become a bird
fly high on dreams
some of them may be of roots

5. Speaking Daggers

Today my words speak daggers
dripping blood they leave a trail
this is where they were
no denial of their crimes
A heart pierced, even twice
a throat cut
an eye gored
bad words doing havoc
killing at sight
even lurking in shadows
planning bloodshed
smiling a false glee

6. A Stone in the River

She stands on a stone in the middle of the river
sticking out her tongue she drinks in the world
each rounded drop a planet in its own right
falling from above
shooting up from beneath
each and one of them quite new to this world
as is she
a child of five, but ready to make her impact
actually, a conqueror in disguise

Her tongue speaks out for her
singing, humming, sucking in
what it says is: This is life!

Was that the moment she slipped and fell?
That very moment, never to be lived again?
A moment lost and turned into eternity?
And she?
She nearly drowned, was rescued, got scolded
"survived" it was called
so she got wet, lost faith and grew "normal"
all in one second
she is never to stand on a stone in the river again

7. Echoes

Echoes go so well with lives
with love, with fates
even with humanities
no more heavyhanded clue than an echo
shall – shall not
love – love not

Love to the drums of doom
success – failure, success – failure
all of it echoes
been there, done that
too old to un-remember former loves
those memories cost heavy duties
all of them love-killers

8. Midgets of Former Times

Midgets, all of them
swarming the place
multiplying everywhere
fornicating the planet to destruction

yes, that's vermin
most of them set out to destroy
none of them anything, but soap bubbles
airy ghosts of former times called beliefs
blow them to pieces and they are reborn
here they are and here they stay
shackles clinging in their pockets

9. Dancing the Nonloving Dance

Did I do the Polka of nonloving?
I'm not sure, but my feet keep dancing
tapping the tune to this out of love–dance
very nicely done, by the way

10. Blotted Out

What am I in light?
The same as in shadows?
Who keeps track of the outlines of our personality?

Who answers our questions of life in a fixed state?
Maybe someone who himself swims in airlessness
who dives into oceans of knowledge
never to return with the answers?

Oh, the light will blot out our shadows
the shadows will hide our light
what's worse we shall never know it happened

11. Just Life

Nowhere
Everywhere
always and never
Oh, you know, that's just life
nothing we can do about it

12. Allow Me to Suggest

Allow me to suggest another life
one that shines in darkness
one that rings out in noisy rooms
one that sets out the beauty of ugliness

Allow me to suggest another love
one that loves when it's needed
one that makes you feel your feelings
one that brings out even more love

Allow me to suggest a new sense of gifts
all of them were for you
all of them brought you blessings
all of them were what they didn't seem to be

Allow me to be
don't underestimate what isn't you
don't see enemies in friends and lovers
don't turn your back on the future

13. Discussion

I want to be loved for my soul, you say
my personality and thoughts, not my body

So your perfect body isn't your soul? I say
Your buttocks dancing rhumba – and whatever?
Your arms and shoulders lifting heavy objects?
Your hands handling objects – and whatever?
That isn't you?

It's my body, not my soul, you say, looking stern
Oh, I say, but your soul lives in your body

14. Hauntings

Gone, they said, gone forever
No coming back, they said
No–no–no never again
that is, except as a ghost

Do I want that?
Want to see your dear face an unmovable mask?
To see your beloved frame grown threadbare?

But what if your eyes are still yours?
Lovely and loving?
Still portals to a soul worth loving?

Then I say: Haunt me
yes, haunt me by day or by night
let the seal between us be your glance
your eyes
the portal to Eternity

15. In the End

In the end it came together
all together, all like one
one flash of insight
one flash of regrets
call it the answer
the ultimate knowledge
or simply "too late"

16. Listing My Life

Listing my life
making an inventory
that's the way to perfection
no disorderliness
all of it lined up on the shelf
nothing lacking
except what was lost in fires
or put on exhibit and sold in a sale

17. Love Mockery

One shouldn't love where hatred rules
harboring what's not love
living pierced feelings of false fulfillment
a sad victory dangling from your belt
nothing but a trophy to hatred
knowing that feeling and still seeking love
that's siding with hatred
turning love into mockery

18. Once a tree

An oak
a giant in the woods
now a stub
a root deep down into secret caves
no birds anymore
plumages nothing but a memory
all visitors blind and naked
worms, maybe munching roots
maybe munching dead animals
none of them sings

19. Manna From Heaven

Manna from heaven
all of it mine
showering me in golden rays
how come when my neighbour starves?
No Manna fell on him
nothing
all of it mine

Bathed in golden rays
nourished like no one else
this Manna embellishes my world
sets me apart, a queen of riches
Standing in my country of golden rays I look out
this outer world is dark and hunger–ridden
myneighbour is crying in fear and pain

I try to give him of my Manna, but in vain
all of it has grown stale
the fickle Heaven took back what it gave
why, I ask, why give and take
why me and not someone else?
No answers in this world of riddles

20. Love in a Parcel

The mailman brought it
oh yes, the parcel came by mail
it looked like any other postal missile
nothing special
just my name in plain writings
– and yours, of course
what a strange outcome of love
now it's detained within a parcel sent by mail
Yes, that's what it comes down to
a love story contained and kept prisoner
held within a cubicle of less than 20 inches

Anyway, we always felt hampered
now I see why

21. A Well Done Hatred

Above the rim of Reality
beneath Nothingness
floating in Space
that's where I found you

All of it came true
as predicted, all of it hard work
no idyll
no rest
not even pleasure

Maybe I came to hate you?
Or did you do the hating game by yourself?
Hatred there was and hatred there is
quite idyllic and restful, by the way
a well done hatred holds pleasures like love

22. With A Dash of God

With a dash of God it's life
Come on, take part, live what's yours
evermore and evermore yours
With a dash of nothing it's whatever you chose
come on, don't be shy, do what you like
keep doing it until you hear that whisper:
"I'm here, where are you?"
Feel it, yes, feel it like a tremor up your spine
know what you knew all along: You are a soul

23. A Certain Kind of Revival

New openings are what she wants
engulfed in dreams of another beginning
each of them sprouts thousand greedy mouths
snapping, hungry for more
flashing teeth ready to tear into life

What could it be?
Passion?

No, hope of even more
a red–hot hope of living against hope
breathing, kissing, devouring life
all of it reborn hopes of a revival
something that turn the spirit high
making it fly like a kite
maybe never to return
never crashing
never being tied down in oblivion

Up there in the sky
her feet flapping in thin air
free of the ground that gave her foothold ...

24. Robber-Dreams

Gone, they said, gone forever
– voices in the dark spoke out
all of them muffled, whispering or hissing
still, they spoke out

Gone where? she asked
Into oblivion, into nowhere–neverland
But they owe me, she yelled in despair
they never gave me anything
Give you? They came to take, to rob

Somewhere there was a faint giggle
Oho, the voices said, they found a victim!
She screamt to feel her pockets being emptied
Oh dear, the voices said, don't fret, you were warned
some dreams and hopes may comfort, still they rob

25. Love of Spiders

"My dear," she said
"love me to death do us depart"
"Ohhhh .,.." he yelled in terror
"No need for that," she said
biting into his thigh
"this is love at first sight"
Three–four gulps and the nuptials were over

So this is love, he thought, passing away
for this I was born, but what about **me**?
I'm a person, I'm a soul, much more than meat
Being digested he was desired, even loved
after that he went into oblivion
a place that turned out to be nice and cosy
a place full of nothingness and many other wonders

26. Reality Lost in Dreams:

A newbie, a starry-eyed believer in new beginnings
in some contents a middle-aged virgin
her reality encompassed in golden dreams
all of them ghosts from a youth spent in hibernation

All she knows is to turn to HIM, the gentle one
his arms are her haven, but not the anchorage of her
dreams
out of the dreams his lips form her resurrection centre
kissing him makes her brave
brave enough to dream of other men
those with cold hearts and greedy lips
those who move like dancers
or maybe bull fighters
those sexy ones with talkative hips
hands like silken dressed claws
the romance guys moving like whips

Her demands to Fate is that all of it comes to her at last
gives her imagined passions she never experienced
what doesn't count are the realities
her youth was lived behind shutters of female virtues
years went by in well behaved wifehood
dangers and darkness never crossed her path
still, beckoning her starving heart
all of it became hers in dreams and hopes

27. Sisyfos

Never ending hillsides
steep deathtraps
she climbs them, one by one
Sisyfos is her guide
he preaches the importance of setting goals

She is set on her dreams of the end station
her true home
dreams of that final destination lure her on
steeper and steeper hillsides beckon her
seemingly all of them dead ends
still, brave and resilient she climbs on
Should she have a medal for being brave?
The medal is hers no matter what
so are the gongs
measuring her progress in heavy heartbeats
tainted instruments, resounding as she climbs

28. I'm A Lasso

To tell you the truth
I'm a lasso
a perfect airborn noose
moved like a whip
stings like a bee
somehow it always finds its target
This vibrant lump of love called YOU

29. She Dances With Hearts

Don't fret, she said, but I dance with hearts
they come to me like stray cats
hungry for love
hungry for fondling
some are, all in all, just hungry

And I, I kiss and fondle them to bits
to tiny fragments
to molecules of molecules
this way they multiply
each fragment a new heart
each heart a new dance
their beatings go like the wings of captured birds
drumming us into ecstacy

III. The Weird World of Reality: Ezine-Articles

The Ugly Duckling and His Discarded Sister

One of the most famous Danes of all times is the writer Hans Christian Andersen (1805-1875). He owes his fame to his talent for writing fairy tales with a point. In reality he was a much more versatile writer as he also published novels and plays for grown-ups. He himself must have felt the need to strike that fact as he is quoted for having said that the parents of his prime readers, i.e. the children, also would find something worthwhile in his stories. Perhaps he felt a little worm of disappointment gnaw at his pride because his fame was based on stories for children and not on his works for grown-ups even though they were considered quite outstanding?

What also gnawed at his system was the thought of his half-sister – or "his mother's daughter" as he called this sibling, Karen Marie Danielsdatter Rosenvinge (1799–1846). They might have been able to brighten each other's lives had they been friends, but no, he could not bring anything that natural over his heart – and his pride. In his opinion she was a disgrace to him and the seemingly mild writer, even writing devotional fairy tales for children, never was happy to see her or to hear of her.

Could the reason for this be that she, being the eldest by six years, had bullied him in the childhood? Well, most of her childhood she, being the daughter of a man who was never married to her mother, was fostered out and only lived with the family for a short period of time. The mother of both the children, Karen Marie and Hans Christian, also was born an illicit child and she was reputed to be a good person so why could her son not accept his sister who started out in the same social position as their mother? It is safe to say that he never accepted this sister and that he suspected her of living an immoral and thus disgraceful life.

In the article "H.C. Andersen's halvsøster, Karen Marie Rosenvinge, og hendes slægt" (: "The half–sister of Hans Christian Andersen, Karen Marie Rosenvinge, and her family") by Bent Østergaard and Kenneth V. Jørgensen it is stated once and for all that there is nothing on her in police archives of that time. Or put another way: Karen Marie was not a prostitute and thus a disgrace to her family, she was a hard working washer woman like their mother. Most likely she was sent out to work as a servant at the tender age of 9–10 years and even though she was very upset when she could not have the address of her brother when he set out from his home as a child to try his luck in Copenhagen she did not pester him with messages or attempts to visit him. The few times he accepted to communicate with her was through the fiancé or maybe even husband of her. It seems that only once did she let into his home and all the noticed was that she looked quite good and younger than her age.

When she died she was all alone and she was buried in the same cemetery as her brother several years later, but nobody knows where her grave is positioned. I often go to the cemetery and had I known where her last resting place is I would have loved to visit it as I see her as a wronged woman, someone who didn't get the chances she might have had.

When Women Were Punished for Being Women

This crime, as I see it, against a certain group of Danish women stemmed from the ideas of Eugenics. However, it also was fed by obsolete ideas of women, morals and sexuality. In both cases it was an attempt to keep society free of "degenerate individuals" by which was meant people who suffered from inherent illnesses, especially of a mental character. The so-called experts felt that letting these "sub-humans" breed would be to endanger society and that had to be stopped at all costs.

It happened in the beginning of the 1900th century, but officially it didn't stop until 1961 when the infamous habit of interring women who were considered "retards" ended. Up til then the morally suspects – i.e. the so-called "lose" women – ended up on the small island of Sprogø. Men convicted of more common crimes than being "lose" were sent to another island by the name of Livø. The main reason for this cruelty was the wish to protect the society at large against "bad, defected genes". Being classified as "immoral" also was a goodbye to the dreams of having children as it would take a fierce fight which they were bound to lose. They might dream, but their reality was that they were not let lose from the island without being sterilized and those of them who already had children most often lost the right to see them. Also because these children were put up for adoption and were expected to break off connections with their presumably immoral and thus degenerate mothers.

Some of these women left the island on their own, but that might cost them their lives: They set out on an attempt to escape by swimming. However, none seems to have succeeded in this dangerous exploit. What is so sad is that what earned the women the name of "retarded" was their lifestyle. To be a woman and to have lovers was seen as an indication that they were mentally defective. It is a backward way of thinking rooted in old fashioned ideas about women and sexuality. One's wish to think that this happened several hundred years back in time is assailed by facts: It did not end until 1961 which means 9 years before the Danish, feminist movement, the "Redstockings" started their actions which went on into the late 1980'ies.

One may wonder at the reasons why these women were considered fitting inmates of an island like Sprogø. However, what brought them there didn't differ from some men's life style and a man who had a child out of wedlock was not interred the way a woman was likely to be. And it is ironic that the island sometimes swarmed with men visiting it in the hope of meeting some of these presumably easy women. Nobody seems to have thought that someone setting sail and venturing out on an erotic expedition to meet immoral women was just as "bad" as they were supposed to be for less.

Dying Twice, One Time Murdered and Buried Alive ...

Did you ever think about which way to die would be the worst one? I don't think I did, but brooching the matter now I feel that the worst kind of death might very well be to be considered dead, only to wake up in the coffin – and be alive.

As if that wasn't enough one has to die once more, i.e. by suffocation as nobody knows about the mistake. Or what about being buried, but then wake up, realize what's going on, beg for one's life and then be clubbed to death? I think that's the very worst scenario I can imagine. Sadly enough that may very well be an accourate account of what happened when the young and exceedingly wealthy widow, Giertrud Birgitte Bodenhoff, died in Copenhagen in 1798.

Now she lies in a stately burial vault or burial chamber on the same churchyard where you'll find the much plainer graves of Hans Christian Andersen and Søren Kierkegaard. According to rumours she doesn't much like her last resting place as some people have reported meeting a very sad, mourning figure by her grave whom they take to be her grieving spirit.

As to what happened it all started when she married her relative, the very affluent merchant and ship owner Andreas Bodenhoff, in 1796. At that time she was only 16 years old and half a year after the wedding she became the richest widow of Europe at the demise of her husband. Sadly enough, young as she is, she herself got very ill from an abscess inside her ear. Nobody can do anything about it, but the pain is excruciating so she is treated with heavy doses of morphine. Apparently the doctors have been a little too generous with this dangerous pain killer because she too died – or did she?

It was much more difficult to establish the death of somebody in 1796 than in our times and Giertrud Birgitte's older brother is worried as his "dead" sister is lying in her coffin looking as rosy as she did before her "death". That's not normal and what's more, the low level of hygiene at that time may have rendered it difficult to discern the smell of death (: putrefaction) from the lack of soap and water so now the question is: Was she dead or wasn't she?

However there are no definite answers to that question, but some years later the truth may have been disclosed when the head gravedigger, Christian Meisling, calls for the priest. He is dying and wants to confess something which by now has become a myth: In 1804 he and the other gravediggers were exposed for their foul habits on the churchyard. Being poor they needed cheap wood for their fires and free clothes on their backs and both these objects (as well as a lot more) they found in the new graves. So they dug up the newly buried corpses and robbed them of everything. Presumably this also happened to Giertrud Birgitte, but when the gravedigger tore off her very valuable ear rings the abscess in her ear burst – and she woke up.

At first she didn't understand what was happening, but when she grasped the situation she begged him to save her life. She offered money and rewards of all kind, but the gravedigger dared not let her live because they knew each other, perhaps from her husband's funeral. The only solution he saw was to kill her so he either clubbed her to death or strangled her and then he buried her once more.

Now, one should notice that her grave wasn't in the ground, but in a burial chamber sitting on the ground and according to theory that's the reason why she may have survived – IF that's what she did.

Many have doubted this story about survival in the grave, but in 1952 the case was investigated and then it was found that the corpse didn't lie in the same position as it was put in 1798 as her feet seemed to have moved. That fact has been taken as an indication that she really did survive, but only to meet her death once more and in a very sad manner.

The Danish Prophet of An Alternate Religion

Martinus Thomsen was born on the 11th of August 1890 as the natural son of a woman who never disclosed the name of his father. He grew up with his foster parents on a small farm, never had any education except for elementary school. As he did not have the financial funds to become a school teacher which was his wish as a young man he became a farm hand, a diary worker, a steward, an office clerk, a postman, etc., etc. as chance would it. He himself felt that all of these different kinds of jobs gave him insight into various areas of life – and that's what life was about to him.

In 1921 when he was 31 years old he had an enlightening experience on an undisclosed day in the month of March. Some would call it a dream and others may see it as a hallucination, but to him it was his cosmic baptism. The event was as follows: He sat alone, focusing on God, when all of a sudden he had what he himself called "a divine calling". Somehow a special information was disclosed to him from somewhere: He was told to use his intuition to explain the cosmic truth which not even Jesus had been able to disclose to his fellow men for the lack of scientific knowledge of his times. Everything which Martinus said or wrote – and that was a lot – he considered a follow-up on the Bible. However, his sayings or writings differed so much from the Christian scripts that in reality he has written something that may be called a new Bible.

As to his earth shaking experience in 1921 he always claimed that it had the bearings of a cosmic vision: "...The vision of Christ that I experienced was not a dream or a hallucination, but a fully awake, day–conscious cosmic experience, and it contained a distinct declaration of a mission that I was to carry out." From that moment he really was on a mission, never to return to the path of the ordinary church teachings. To him his mission was the obligation to show people God and to teach them about Jesu mission.

He had – and still has – many followers and today they connect in the Martinus Institute where they discuss his many works and his "Cosmology" which reads that the Universe is an all–embracing and living being. We are here solely for the experience of life itself which is supposed to develop and refine us over time when we have been born and reincarnated many, many times. In the end we shall have refined all senses and also have developed new instincts and new abilities. However, Martinus is not widely known outside of Scandinavia, even though he has published many books like e.g. his main work "The Book of Life" which is also called "The Third Testament".

When he died he was put to rest in a rich mausoleum which outraged some people who thought that he had grown haughty and tried to put himself out to be more exalted than everyone else. Those people can't have known his teachings very well as his reason for this luxurious burial place was his belief that humans hold an obligation toward all the small animal organisms that live in their bodies and which should have time to find other lodgings, so to speak. To him we are all part of Cosmos as such, but we also constitute a Cosmos to other living creatures.

The Child Crusaders

The Medieval crusaders have been seen as someone very brave, courageous and honorable. Also, we tend to forget that we (the Christian part of the world) didn't come out victorious. No, far from it ...

One of the episodes which is quite impossible to forget even today is the French and German Children's Crusades in 1212. The first one was instigated by a 12 year old shepherd-boy called Stephen (or Etienne). He approached the French king Philip and handed him "a letter from Jesus" whom he said had appeared to him while he was tending the sheep. Presumably Jesus had ordered him to go and preach the Crusades to the public. Now, the king didn't believe him or wasn't too impressed by him, but he himself was undismayed by this fact and started to preach wherever he had a chance to bring out the message to someone.

Actually, he seems to have been an oral genius who caught the attention of a lot of people – and circa 20–30,000 thousand children who wanted to follow him. Some of these children were of noble birth and they had run away from their wealthy homes to join his "army" of children. At Marseilles two merchants, Hugh the Iron and William the Pig, offered them ships, free of charge – and from then on nobody knew anything about their fate for a very long time. Actually, they disappeared and were not to be seen or heard of for 18 years.

However, in Germany a boy by the name of Nicholas entered on the same course. He and his cohorts – also many girls – set out on their way to Palestine in order to free Jerusalem, but the losses were heavy, due to starvation and other hardships. When many of them gave up their plans to go to Palestine they were too exhausted to go back home, but decided to stay where they were, i.e. in Italy. Others set out to cross the Alps to get back home. However, some of the dead children's parents were so enraged by Nicholas, who by this time had disappeared, that they took his aged father and hanged him.

As to Stephen's company who had set out in three ships then two of these vessels were shipwrecked and all aboard drowned. This the families of the children learned when a young priest returned home to Europe after 18 years of captivity in a Muslim country. He told that those on the third ship were taken to Muslim slave markets and they learnt the hard way that those two merchants who had proposed to help them actually had set them up for sale. They were betrayed by them, but some years later they in their turn were hanged for attempting to kidnap the Emperor Frederick. Some of the sold Christian children were killed for not being willing to accept Islam, but others were lucky enough to be bought by the governor of Egypt, al-Kamil, who treated them very kindly and who set them to work as interpreters, teachers, etc. without demanding that they became Muslims.

All in all these sad stories of committed, but betrayed children should be better investigated than they are. Most of them are mere myths, but it's a historical fact that these groups of children set out as crusaders just as did the grown-ups.

The Murderer Who Changed His/Her Sex

In 1893 there was an immense scandal of dimensions in Copenhagen. The lady superintendent of the home for wayward or orphaned boys, KANA, i.e. Vilhelmine Møller, confessed to having murdered one of the orphans. The unlucky boy was the 15 year old Volmer Sjøgren and her reason to take his young life was that they had been lovers so that he unfortunately had learned her most well guarded secret, namely the fact that in reality "she" was a he or perhaps a hermaphrodite.

Vilhelmine Møller's sexual organs had been deformed ever since birth. However, when she/he was arrested and taken to prison she/he also underwent a medical examination and her/his sex was determined as masculine. Even today the case is not quite clear, but as her (his) organs were more masculine than female she (he) now officially became a man and had the name of Vilmelmine Møller changed into Frederik Vilhelm Schmidt which means that the "she"/"he" of this article is now turning into a "he".

As to the crime it was almost incomprehensible that he would harm any of the boys as he had been an outstanding and very considerate superintendent who also published articles about his advanced ideas for the education of these forlorn children. Perhaps his good reputation as a dedicated head master is the reason why his former – and very mysterious – assistant, Mrs.Mackwitz, was seen by the public as the one who had corrupted his morals, in a way thus being the true criminal. However, blaming her did not blot out the sad fact that he was a murderer and he concurrently was sentenced to death. This sentence was eventually changed into imprisonment for life, but as early as 1905 he was released and that same year he married. It seems that from then on he lead a good and to all intents normal life with his wife.

In 1906 he published a short article about his life in a magazine, "Naturen og Mennesket" (: "Nature and the Human Being"). He died on Christmas Eve in 1936 at the ripe old age of 91. One of the reasons this sad murder was such a scandal was that at that time these special homes for the orphaned children were run by private donations. All the people who were engaged in this work feared that they would lose the public support which was the foundation of the homes, but that did not happen. The public did not lose sympathy with these young outcasts or the people who tended and educated them. On the contrary, they went on supporting them until 1905 when the homes became part of a special children's act and thus turned State wards. Up till then they had lived at the mercy and sympathy of the public.

DIGTEREN

HANS CHRISTIAN
ANDERSEN

The Handsome Corpse

The dead body of the Tollund Man is in itself a strange miracle because it is so very well preserved. It has been said that he is the best preserved corpse in the world even though he has been dead since around 500 BC. The reason why this dead man is considered handsome even today is that it's still possible to discern fingerprints, beard stubbles, facial features as well as facial expression. One thing is for sure he is amazing in the way his looks exhibit an inner peace and tranquility even in his cruel death by hanging. There is no panic to be seen in this face of a man who supposedly was the sacrificial gift to some god or goddess. His fellow men treated him with respect and there are no marks on him that indicate he should be a criminal who was executed for some crime. In his stomach there was found the remains of a gruel of 30 different plant seeds. No traces of meat.

Actually dead bodies were cremated in the early Iron Age, only the bog people have been buried in this way. Nobody really knows why. Close by the spot where the Tollund Man was found another bog body had been found in 1938, i.e. the Elling woman, who also had been hanged at around the same time. However, she is not at all as well preserved as him and does not bear the same expression of serenity. To find a corpse as fine looking as the Tollund man we should go to e.g. Greenland where some have been found frozen by the permafrost.

The reason why these finds make such an impression isn't that they are dead people, but that they, so to speak, are visitors from the past. Their faces tell us much about the people whom we stem from.

http://www.youtube.com/watch?v=5CQE4c8UJkM&feature=player_embedded
http://www.youtube.com/watch?v=gZHPYmfwUxA

The Man Who Loved Unicorns

The museum of Ole Worm (1558–1654) was the very first museum in Denmark. It was filled with every kind of exotica from old fossils to stuffed animals and a large part of these objects exists even today. As he was obsessed by collecting artifacts of all kinds his museum is rich in details. Nothing seems too little or too shallow for him. For instance, he was interested in lemmings and succeeded in establishing the fact that they were in truth rodents. The old, alternate opinion, which still was very popular, was that they simply generated from air. Another old myth that concerned him was the one about the birds of paradise which were supposed not to have any feet. Once again he proved that the myth did not tell the truth as they indeed had feet. This he did by drawing them.

However, his most illustrious exploit was the one of unicorns. The legend went that they were magical animals, but he determined that they did not exist which was quite logical as nobody had ever seen them. He also established the truth that their famed, magical horns were nothing but narhwhal tusks. Strangely enough he himself could not shake off some other superstitious beliefs about unicorns. One of them was that the horns of these admittedly non-existent animals could heal people when poisoned. To prove that the legend spoke the truth he set out to poison pets and then feeding them ground-up narhwal tusks in order to save them. According to his reports they did indeed survive being poisoned when fed narhwal tusks.

Perhaps it is this experiment which earned him H.P. Lovecraft's interest and turned him into his notorious character Olaus Wormius who was set to translate the "Grimoire the Necronomicon" from Arabic into Latin. This literary character is rather creepy, which Ole Worm doesn't seem to have been.

When he died from a bladder–disorder his rich collection of exotica was sold to the Danish king, Frederik III, who turned it into the basis for "The Royal Kunstkammer". This collection of historical artifacts may still be seen today as part of the very fine and interesting Zoological Museum in Copenhagen.

Viking Love, Rape and Incest

All of us know that the old Vikings of Scandinavia were cruel and brutal warriors because that's what we have been told. Their image is somewhat troll like according to the way they have been depicted in modern times. However, in the Sagas, i.e. the medieval prose narratives of Scandinavian gods and heroes, they are first and foremost heroic and very brave figures. To these men it is no crime to set out on a predatory expedition as it is part of their obligations to restore order according to their beliefs. They conquer land which they feel belong to them and they kill enemies because that is necessary to obtain this goal. Some of their expeditions have a religious background as they want to serve their own gods by destroying those who are not part of their pantheon.

One of the most renowned warrior–heroes is the Danish Viking Helge, the brother of king Roar. In some of the sagas he seems to have died a very young man, but in others, like in the "Skjoldungesaga–fragment" he lives and he sure is a very active Viking. His fate is to be known and remembered as the Viking who raped the proud Olof who was married to a Saxon earl and who had derided him. However, this revenge, as it is called, leads to the birth of a daughter who is kept a secret by her mother and is so hated by her that she names her after her dog, i.e. Yrsa.

Several years after the birth of Yrsa her father, Helge, who still doesn't know anything about her, returns to the scenery for the rape and this time he abducts the beautiful, young girl and brings her with him to Denmark where he marries her. Strangely enough this marriage becomes a success. Both of them are unaware of the incest they are committing and are happy when their son, Rolf Krake, is born. But now the vengeful Olof strikes out to destroy their illicit happiness by informing them of their close relationship. The unhappy Yrsa leaves the Danish court and she marries the Swedish King Adils who later tries to murder Helge and also Rolf. However, Helge lives to have another daughter, Skuld, by a woman who is set out to be some kind of a fairy. This daughter proves to be quite different from Yrsa as she is cruel by nature and quite demonic. She plays one of the main parts in the killing of her brother, Rolf Krake.

At that point Rolf Krake had grown to become one of the most renown heroes of the Viking sagas. He is even supposed to have been one of the very early kings of Denmark, but as with his father, that's more than unlikely. Actually, both of them may just be fictive characters in the Viking sagas of Scandinavia. Besides that, Helge is mixed up with other brave, famous and also fierce Vikings of that name.

Karen Blixen's Alias Isak Dinesen's Shadowy Aide, Her Secretary Clara Selborn

Clara Selborn (born Svendsen: 1916) was the secretary of the famous Danish writer Karen Blixen (pen name Isak Dinesen) who e.g. wrote "Seven Gothic Tales" (1934), "Out of Africa" (1937/38), "Winter's Tales" (1942/43) and "Last Tales" (1957). In a way Clara was a very famous person as she was known as the shadowy secretary who however, played an important role in the life of the famous writer. Many wondered at her personality because Clara, who always was her own person, lived by her own rules. I knew her quite well as we were friends for many years until we sadly enough fell out. However, even though we did not meet after that we corresponded until she died on the 1st of April 2009.

What set Clara apart was her strong idealism. She wanted to find a cause or a person to serve. In Karen Blixen she found both, but before that happened she had tried to attain the role of a serving spirit with someone else who turned her down, maybe because there was some suspicions that she was out to secure herself a husband. Actually, Clara had, as she told me, long ago chosen never to marry, but only live for the causes she believed in.

Karen Blixen was her main cause, but another one was Lord Byron whom she admired very much, a third one was Israel and the Jewish people and still another one was the Catholic Church. When I asked her why she, as the only one in her family, had become a Catholic her answer was that it was because of the beautiful and colorful liturgy. To me that was a strange answer as I was much more into ideas and ideologies than that kind of outward manifestations of a religious faith. I felt the same about Lord Byron whose poetry I didn't find very deep, but she enjoyed the sheer beauty of it.

After Karen Blixen's death in 1962 she became the literary executor of her works. That meant that it was her responsibility to see to it that the best agreements were obtained when they were republished or translated into another language. Also she became a member of the committee of Rundstedlundfondet (The Foundation of Rungstedlund) which furnished her with yet another kind of responsibility. To make ends meet she also worked as a translator, e.g. of some of the Blixen-scripts that were published in Danish after the death of the writer. However, the main bulk of her many translations was of Graham Greene, but the one she considered her flagship, so to speak, was Tomasi di Lampedusa's "The Leopard". When it got translated by someone else several years later she became very upset as well as disappointed, also because her translation was considered outstanding.

She also wrote her autobiography, "Notater om Karen Blixen" (1974: Not translated, except into German) and collaborated in several works about Karen Blixen and her writings.

Death in An Apartment House

The old man who was found exactly one year after his death was almost blind and he did not mix with anybody so only his neighbors and the people living in the flat beneath his knew the common sounds from his daily life. For instance, did he watch television, did he walk his floor in a noisy manner and what about the telephone? It appears that those who lived in the flat below his one had tried to make the janitor investigate the uncanny silence, the new reality of a no–sound–situation in his flat. However, when nobody answered the door bell he took for granted that the almost blind, old man didn't want anyone visiting so he stopped his "investigation" into the matter. I think that was the moment when he should have called the police, but he did not want to bother this old and sick man with professional investigations.

Nevertheless, investigations there were once again when the warm weather set in and the house suddenly was swarmed with insects. When that happened the dead and by now more or less skeletonized man was detected. The newspapers wrote indignant articles about the case and that way we, the other inhabitants of the house, also learnt that this incident was not all that rare. Actually, many people were found days, weeks or even months after their death. These people were also those who did not have any funeral procession of friends and family as they most likely didn't have either anymore.

An even worse case was of a man who was found in his flat no less than five years after his death.

Now that is crazy as five years is not like not seeing someone for a week or two. Obviously this dead man's relatives or friends did not miss him so it must be concluded that he had neither. He too was a pensioner living off his pension and nobody noticed that he did not withdraw as much money as he used to. Also nobody wondered at the heaps of newspapers, magazines and advertising pamphlets by his door. Neither did anybody pay attention to the stench of death which must have oozed from his closed front door. Here we have a case of a human being who must have been invisible all his life and who was treated as non-existing even before his death. That is very, very sad, but as stated by the newspapers not all that uncommon these days.

Both these cases – and all other cases like them – are embarrassing to the dead man's immediate neighborhood. One must wonder at this common absence of consideration for a fellow human being. The fact that someone may lie undetected in a building swarming with people and not being found for five years is almost unfathomable. The same goes for the other case as one year is long too. One week or so may be understandable with people living by themselves, but neither five nor "only" one years. I really think that we are obliged to pay attention to signs of illness or death close by. That is our duty as the good neighbor we all should be in an ideal society.